Junie B. Jones
and some
Sneaky Peeky Spying

By Barbara Park

Illustrated by Denise Brunkus

Chicken House

2 Palmer Street, Frome, Somerset BA11 1DS

The Junie B. Jones series by Barbara Park

To my editor, Linda Hayward –
Junie B.'s bestest real-life friend

First published in the United States in 1994 by Random House, Inc.
Text copyright © 1994 by Barbara Park
Illustrations copyright © 1994 by Denise Brunkus

This edition first published in Great Britain in 2006 by
The Chicken House
2 Palmer Street
Frome, Somerset BA11 1DS
United Kingdom
www.doublecluck.com

Cover design by Radio
Cover Illustration by Denise Brunkus
Typeset by Dorchester Typesetting Group Ltd
Printed in the UK by CPI Bookmarque, Croydon, CR0 4TD

3 5 7 9 10 8 6 4

British Library Cataloguing in Publication data available.

13 digit ISBN 978 1 905294 09 1

Contents

Chapter 1

Sneaky Peeky Spying

My name is Junie B. Jones. The B stands for Beatrice. Except I don't like Beatrice. I just like B and that's all.

At school, I'm in Reception. Reception is what comes before Year One. Except for I don't know why it's called that silly word of Reception. 'Cos it should be called Year Zero, I think.

My teacher has the name of Mrs.

She has another name, too. But I just like Mrs and that's all.

Mrs has short brown hair. And long skirts of wool. And she smiles a real lot.

Except for sometimes when I'm noisy, she claps her loud hands at me.

It used to scare me very much. Only then I got used to it. And now I don't even pay it any attention.

I wish Mrs lived next door to me.

Then me and her would be neighbours.

And bestest friends.

And also I could spy on her.

Spying is when you be very quiet. And you look at people through a peeky hole or a crack or something.

I am a very good spier.

That's because I have sneaky feet. And my nose doesn't whistle when I breathe.

Last Friday morning at Grampa Miller's house, I hided in the dirty clothes basket.

Then my grampa came in the bathroom.
And I lifted up the lid a teeny bit. And I
peeked my eyes at him.

And guess what?

Grampa Miller took his whole teeth right
out of his head! That's what!

I popped right out of the basket!

"HEY! GRAMPA! HOW DID YOU DO THAT AMAZING THING?" I shouted.

Then my grampa screamed very loud. And he runned out of the bathroom speedy quick.

Grampa Miller has high blood pressure, I think.

Pretty soon Mother hurried into the bathroom with angry feet.

"That's it!" she yelled. "No more spying! This is the last time I'm telling you! Do you hear me, madam? Do you?"

"Yes," I said. "'Cos you're shouting right in my ear, that's why."

Then Mother took me home. Except for she kept on staying mad at me.

"Find something quiet to do," she said kind of growly. "Your baby brother has to take his morning nap."

So then I thought and thought about what to do. And a very great idea popped into my head.

First, I took off my loud shoes . . .

Then I tippy-toed into baby Ollie's room in just my sock feet . . .

And I spied on him through the bars of his cot.

'Cos what could be quieter than sneaky peeky spying, of course!

Only too bad for me. Because that boring old baby just kept on sleeping and sleeping.

And he wasn't being fun.

So that's how come I accidentally blowed on his face.

And I tickled his nose with a ribbon.

And I shouted, "WAKE UP!" in his ear.

And guess what? Ollie opened his eyes, that's what!

Then he started crying very loud. And Mother runned into his room.

Only she didn't even see me!

'Cos I quick hided in the wardrobe!

I smiled to just myself. I'm the bestest

spier in the whole wide world, I said inside my head.

That's how come – when I went on the mini-bus to school that day – I did a little bit of bragging.

"I'm the bestest spier in the whole world," I said to my bestest friend named Grace.

Then I took off my shoes. And I showed her my sneaky sock feet.

"See?" I said. "See how quiet they are? You can hardly even hear these things."

After that, I breathed in and out for her.

"And see? My nose doesn't whistle, either," I said.

That Grace smiled. "I'm good at spying, too," she said.

I patted her. "Yeah, only too bad, Grace. But you can't be as good as me. 'Cos I said it first."

That Grace did a mad breath at me. It is called a huffy, I think.

"I heard your nose whistle, Grace," I told her.

Just then the bus got to school. And me and that Grace raced each other to the playground.

Except for she beated me. Only it didn't count. 'Cos I wasn't really racing.

Then we played horses with my other bestest friend named Lucille. Only pretty soon the bell rang. And we all runned to Room Nine speedy quick.

Mrs was at the door waiting for us.

"Good afternoon, ladies," she said.

"Good afternoon, lady," I said back very polite.

Then Mrs smiled at me.

That's because she is the nicest teacher

I ever saw.

And so I wish me and her were bestest friends.

And guess what else?

I wish I could hide in her basket.

Chapter 2

Questions

Me and my bestest friend Lucille sit at my same table together.

My table is where I sit up straight.

And do my work.

And don't talk to my neighbour.

Except I keep on forgetting that part.

"I wonder where Mrs lives?" I whispered to Lucille real quiet.

"Shh," said Lucille. "We can't talk or else we'll get in trouble. And anyway, you're not allowed to know where she lives. 'Cos it's a secret."

"Says who?" I asked.

"Says my brother, that's who. And he's in Year Three. And he says teachers have to keep their house a secret. Or else kids might go there and throw rotten tomatoes."

I did a huffy at her.

"Yeah, only I don't want to throw rotten tomatoes, Lucille," I explained. "I just want to hide in her clothes basket, and that's all."

"I don't care," she said. "You're still not allowed. 'Cos my brother said so. And he knows more than you do. So there."

I made an angry face. "*So there* is not a nice word, Lucille," I said.

Then I made a fist at her. Except for Mrs saw me. And so I had to unfold it.

After that I behaved myself very good. I sat up really straight. And I did all my work.

Work is when you use your brain and a pencil.

Only sometimes I accidentally use the rubber too hard. And a big hole rubs in my paper.

"Hey! I did beautifully today!" I called out. "'Cos guess what? No hole! That's what!"

Mrs came to my table. She put a gold star on my work.

"You *did* do beautifully, Junie B.," she said. "Maybe I'll hang this one on the wall for Grandparents' Day on Monday. Would you like that?"

"Yes," I said. "Only I keep on forgetting how come they're coming to this place."

Then Mrs explained to me all about Grandparents' Day again.

She said our grandparents are coming for

a visit. And we get to show them Room Nine. And also we get to have 'freshments together.

Mrs said 'freshments are biscuits and abeverage.

I raised my hand.

"Yeah, only I don't think I'm allowed to have the kind of drink named abeverage. 'Cos I'm only allowed to have milk and juice and that's all."

Mrs looked up at the ceiling with her eyes. Then I looked up there, too. But I didn't see anything.

"How many of you think you can bring biscuits on Monday?" asked Mrs.

"I CAN! I CAN! I yelled very excited. "'COS MY MOTHER IS THE BESTEST BISCUIT BAKER IN THE WHOLE WORLD, THAT'S WHY! EXCEPT FOR ONE TIME SHE ACCIDENTALLY

FORGOT THEY WERE IN THE OVEN. AND THE FIREMEN HAD TO COME TO OUR HOUSE."

Mrs laughed. Only I don't know why. 'Cos that was not a funny story.

After that, she gave me a note for Mother. It was some writing about baking biscuits, I think.

"If your mother has any questions, please tell her to call me," said Mrs.

Just then I got a very great idea!

"Hey!" I said. "Maybe me and Mother can bring the biscuits to your house! And so then I can see where you live!"

Mrs rumpled my hair. "You don't have to come to my house, Junie B. Just bring the biscuits to school on Monday morning."

I smiled very sweet. "Yeah, only I still want to see where you live," I said.

Then Mrs turned around. And she walked back to her desk.

That's how come I had to follow her.

"Do you have the rich kind of house? Or the ordinary kind of house?" I asked her. "'Cos I just have the ordinary kind of house. Except for Mother wants the rich kind. Only Daddy said *you'll be lucky*."

Mrs pointed at my chair. That means to sit down, I think.

"Yeah, only do you have a daddy that lives at your house, too? Are there any pictures of him in your purse? Let's look in there, OK? Do you have a secret compartment in it? 'Cos my Grampa Miller has one of those things with fifty pounds in it. Only don't tell

Grandma."

Mrs took my hand. Then me and her walked back to my table.

"Yeah, only guess what I'm wondering now? Now I'm wondering what your bedtime is. 'Cos my bedtime is when the little hand is at the seven, and the big hand is at the six. Only I hate that stupid bedtime. 'Cos I'm not even tired yet, of course."

Mrs put her finger up to her lips.

"That's enough, Junie B.," she said. "I mean it. I want you to settle down now."

Then she went right back to the front of the room. And she didn't answer any of my questions.

'Cos guess why?

Mrs is a secret mystery person. That's why.

Chapter 3

Secret Mystery Person

Me and my bestest friend Grace went home on the bus together.

That's when I told her about Mrs and her secret house.

"Mrs is a secret mystery person," I said. "'Cos she wouldn't answer any of my questions. And so now I have curiosity about her."

That Grace wrinkled her eyebrows. "Me, too," she said. "Now I have curiosity about her, too."

I patted her again. "Yeah, only too bad,

Grace. But you can't have as much as me. 'Cos I said it first, remember that?"

That Grace did another huffy at me.

"Whoops. Your nose is still whistling, Grace," I said.

A few minutes later, I got off the bus. I runned to my house like a speedy rocket.

"GRANDMA! GRANDMA!" I shouted very excited. "IT'S ME! IT'S JUNIE B. JONES! I'M HOME FROM MY SCHOOL!"

Grandma Miller babysits me and baby Ollie when Mother is at work.

She was in the kitchen feeding Ollie mashed-up peas.

"GUESS WHAT, GRANDMA! GUESS WHAT? MY TEACHER IS A SECRET MYSTERY PERSON! AND SHE WON'T TELL ME WHERE SHE LIVES. ONLY I

WANT TO GO TO HER HOUSE VERY BAD!"

Grandma Miller shushed me. "There's no need to shout, Junie B.," she said. "I'm right here."

"Yeah, only I can't help it, Grandma! 'Cos I have curiosity about her!"

Grandma Miller did a little smile. "Curiosity killed the cat, you know," she said.

Then my mouth went open. And my eyes got very big too.

"What cat, Grandma? Where did the curiosity kill it? Was it in the street by my school? 'Cos I saw a squished cat in the street by my school. Only Paulie Allen Puffer said it got runned over by the ice-cream van."

Grandma Miller looked at me for a very long time. Then she went to the sink. And she took an aspirin.

Just then I heard a noise at the front door.

And its name is Mother was home from work!

"MOTHER! MOTHER! I HAVE A 'PORTANT NOTE FROM MRS. 'COS YOU AND ME ARE GOING TO BAKE DELICIOUS BISCUITS, AND THEN WE CAN TAKE THEM TO HER HOUSE AND SEE WHERE SHE LIVES!"

Mother read the note.

"The note says to take the biscuits to school, Junie B. Not to your teacher's house."

"Yeah, only I already know that. But my teacher is a secret mystery person. And she won't tell me where she lives. And so you and me have to find it ourselves."

Mother shook her head. "No way, sweetie," she said.

"Yes way! I shouted. "We have to! 'Cos

now I've got curiosity in me. And I have to find out where her house is. Or else Grandma said I'm goin' to get runned over by an ice-cream van."

Then Mother did a frown at Grandma. And Grandma took another aspirin.

"Your teacher is *not* a secret mystery person, Junie B.," said Mother. "She's just an ordinary person. With an ordinary family. And there's no way that you and I are going to bother her at her house."

I stamped my foot. "YES, WE ARE! WE ARE TOO! 'COS I WANT TO, THAT'S WHY!"

After that, I got sended to my room.

'Cos of no shouting. And no stamping my foot. Only I never even heard of that stupid dumb rule before.

I shut my door very angry. Then I put my

head under my pillow. And I called Mother the name of pooey head.

"And guess what else?" I said very quiet. "Teachers are not ordinary people.

"So there. Ha ha."

Chapter 4

Biscuit Mix and Other Stuff

The next day was Saturday.

Saturday is the day me and my mother go to the supermarket.

I have rules at that place.

Like no shouting the words I WANT ICE CREAM!

And no calling Mother the name of big meanie when she won't buy it.

And no eating a bag of marshmallows that

doesn't belong to you.

Or else the shop man yanks it away from you. And he says, *Eating is the same thing as stealing, young lady.*

Then he takes you to Mother. And she has to pay for the whole entire bag. Except for I don't know why. 'Cos I only ate three of those softy things and that's all.

The trolleys at the supermarket have seats in them. That's where babies sit. Only not me. 'Cos big girls get to walk all by theirselves.

And guess what else? One time Mother even let me push the whole big trolley without any help.

Except for then some baked beanies got knocked off their shelf. And a grandma got her foot caught in my wheel. And so now I have to wait till I'm bigger.

My favourite aisle is where the biscuits are. That's 'cos sometimes there is a lady at a table there. And she gives me and Mother biscuit samples. And we don't even have to pay for them.

Their name is freebies, I think.

Only too bad for me. 'Cos this time the lady wasn't there.

"Rats," I said very disappointed. "No freebie lady."

Mother smiled. "That's OK. When we get home, we're going to bake our own biscuits for Grandparents' Day, remember? Won't that be fun?" she asked.

I made my shoulders go up and down.

That's 'cos I was still mad at her for not taking me to my teacher's house, of course.

"What kind of biscuit mix do you want?" asked Mother.

I did a frown at her. "I don't even want to bake biscuits any more," I said. "'Cos you still won't take me to where Mrs lives."

Mother rumpled my hair. "Staying cross isn't going to change things, Junie B.," she said. "Now do you want to pick out the biscuit mix? Or shall I?"

Then Mother picked out some biscuit mix. And she gave it to me. And I throwed it in the trolley very hard.

"Thank you," said Mother.

"You're not welcome," I said.

After that, Mother took me outside of the shop. And me and her had a little talk.

A little talk is when Mother is mad at me. And she says who do I think I am, madam? And zactly how long do I think she's going to put up with me?

Then I have to say a 'pology to her.

A 'pology is the words *I'm sorry*.

Except for you don't actually have to mean it. 'Cos nobody can even tell the difference.

After the little talk, we went back into the shop.

"Shall we try again?" asked Mother.

Then she gave me another box of biscuit mix. And I put it in the trolley very nice.

"That's better," she said. "Thank you."

You're not welcome, I said inside my head.

Then I smiled to just myself, 'cos Mother can't even hear me in there.

After that, me and her went around the corner. And I saw my most favourite thing in the whole world!

And its name is the water fountain!

"Hey! I need a drink!" I said very excited.

Then I runned right over there. And I hopped up on the little step.

"Need some help?" called Mother.

"No," I said. "'Cos I'm almost five years old, that's why. And so I already know how to work this thing.

"And here's another thing I know," I said. "No putting your mouth on the water spout. Or else germs will get inside you. And you will die."

I smiled very proud. "Paulie Allen Puffer told me that," I explained.

Then I bended my head over the fountain. And I drank for a very long time.

"Hurry up, Junie B.," said Mother. "I need to get the shopping done."

I wiped my mouth off with my arm.

"Yeah, only I can't hurry up. Or else I might get a stomach ache and sick up water.

'Cos a boy named William did that on the playground yesterday."

Mother looked at her watch. "OK. Well, I'm going to be right here in the cereal aisle. As soon as you've finished drinking, come directly back to me."

"Okey-dokey," I said very happy.

Then I turned around and drinked and drinked and drinked.

Except for then I started feeling a little bit sickish. And so I had to sit down on the little step and rest my water.

That's when the big front doors of the supermarket opened.

And guess what?

My eyes almost popped out of my head, that's what!

'Cos I saw a big shock!

And its name was Mrs!

My real live teacher named Mrs was at the supermarket!!!

Chapter 5

Sickish

Mrs didn't see me.

That's because I hided behind the water fountain speedy fast.

And guess what?

She had a *man* with her!

And I never even saw that guy before!

"Hey! Who on earth is that?" I said to just myself.

Then I runned my fastest to the cereal aisle, to tell Mother what I saw.

Only all of a sudden I remembered about

how she told me *no more spying*. And so maybe I might get in trouble with her, I think.

That's how come I stopped running. And I started to go back to peek at Mrs some more. But Mother already spotted me.

"Hey! Where are you going?" she called at me. "Come here."

"Yeah, only I can't come there," I explained. "'Cos I just remembered something very important. And it's called – I haven't finished drinking yet!"

Then I runned right back to the water fountain. Only Mrs and the strange man were already disappeared.

"Drat," I said. "Where did those sneaky peoples go?"

After that I had to look all over the shop.

First, I looked where the chocolate milk was. Then I looked where the pasta and tomato sauce was. And I also looked where the delicious sweets were.

Only guess where I finally found them?

At the stupid stinky vegetables! That's where!

I quick ducked down and hided around the corner.

Then I did some sneaky peeky spying on them.

I saw Mrs picking out yucky blucky brockly.

And euwie pewie tomatoes.

And also the kind of vegetable named Archie Choke.

Except for then the strange man snatched Archie Choke right out of her hands. And he tried to put it back on the shelf.

Only Mrs grabbed it right back again. And she pretended to hit him on the head with it. And then they both started laughing very much.

That's when a very terrible thing happened.

And it's called – Mrs and the strange man did a big smoochie kiss!

And it was in front of the whole entire everybody!

I covered my eyes. That's 'cos I was 'shamed of her, of course. On account of teachers shouldn't do that smoochie thing!

After that, I peeked my eyes between my fingers. And I saw Mrs standing at the grapes.

She picked up a bunch of the green kind. Then she pulled some grapes right off the top of it.

And that's when the most terrible thing of all happened!

Because just then, Mrs put the grapes in

her mouth!

And she ATE them!

Mrs ATE the GRAPES!

And she didn't even PAY for them!

"Oh no," I whispered very upset. "Oh no. Oh no."

'Cos eating is the same thing as stealing, remember?

And teachers aren't supposed to do stealing! Teachers are supposed to be perfecter than that! 'Cos they have to set a good zample for little children!

After that I felt very sickish inside of my stomach.

On account of Mrs didn't even get caught and learn her lesson!

'Cos nobody saw what she did!

Not the shop man.

Not the strange man.

Nobody.

Nobody except for me.

Chapter 6
Squeezy Lips

I didn't telltale on Mrs.

That's 'cos if I told Mother, I would get in trouble for spying.

And if I told the shop man, Mrs might go to prison.

And so I just kept it a secret inside my head.

'Cos nobody can see secrets inside your head.

Not even if they look in your ears.

On Sunday Grandma and Grampa Miller came to our house for dinner. Only I couldn't talk to them that much.

That's because secrets are very slippery. And I didn't want it to slip out of my mouth by accident.

"Why so quiet tonight, Junie B.?" said Grandma Miller at the table. "Cat got your tongue?"

My mouth went wide open.

"What cat, Grandma? Is it the same cat that got killed by the ice-cream van? How come he wants to get my tongue? Did his tongue get squished in the accident?"

Grandma Miller made a face. Then she didn't eat her roast beef any more.

Mother looked surprised at me. "You're very chatty all of a sudden. Does this mean you're not cross about the biscuits any more?"

And so then I remembered to stop talking again. Or else my secret might slip out.

I squeezed my lips together very tight.

And guess what else? Even the next day – when I was on the bus to school – my lips still stayed squeezed.

"Hi, Junie B.," said my bestest friend Grace.

I did a wave at her.

That Grace frowned at me. "How come you're not saying hi? You *have* to say hi. It's the rules."

Except for I still didn't say hi.

And so then she called me the name of big stinky.

And when we got to school, that Grace told Lucille I was being a meanie. And so those two played horses all by theirselves.

And not me.

That's how come I finally had to sing something very loud at them.

"I'VE GOT A SECRET! HA-HAHA-HA-HAAAA-HAAA," I sang.

That Grace put her hands on her hips.

"So?" she said. "We don't care. Do we, Lucille?"

Except for just then Lucille runned over to me speedy quick. 'Cos she cared, that's why.

"If you tell me your secret, I'll be your best friend," she said.

"Yeah, only I can't, Lucille," I explained. "'Cos if I tell you my secret, Mrs might get in big trouble. And so I have to keep it inside my head."

Lucille did a frown at me.

"It's not good to keep secrets inside your head, Junie B.," she said. "My brother says

keeping secrets inside your head makes pressure in there. And pretty soon your head blows up."

My eyes got very big at her.

"Oh no!" I shouted real upset.

Then I holded my head real tight with my hands. And I runned my very fastest to the nurse's office. 'Cos she has plasters to hold your head together, I think.

"MY HEAD'S GONNA BLOW UP! MY HEAD'S GONNA BLOW UP!" I yelled at the nurse.

She jumped up from her desk and hurried over to me.

"What's wrong, Junie B.? Do you have a bad headache?" she asked.

"No. I have a bad *secret*. It's about Mrs. Only I can't tell anybody! And now there's pressure in my head. And I need a plaster. Or else it's gonna splode!"

The nurse said calm down to me. Then she put a plaster on my head. And me and her went to Headteacher's office.

Headteacher is the boss of the school.

Me and him know each other very good.

That's because I keep on getting sent down there. And so now I'm not even afraid of him.

Headteacher sat me in a big wood chair.

"Good afternoon, Junie B.," he said. "What's the trouble today?"

"Good afternoon," I said back. "My head's gonna blow up."

Headteacher frowned his eyes at me. "Why do you think that?" he asked.

I did a little bit of squirming. "'Cos I got a secret in there, that's why," I said.

Headteacher sat down at his big desk. He folded his hands.

"Maybe if you tell me your secret, I can help you," he said.

"Yeah, only I can't talk," I told him.

Headteacher looked disappointed at me.

"But I thought you and I were friends," he said.

"We are," I said. "I'm not even afraid of you."

Headteacher did a chuckle. "Good. That's good," he said. "Then why don't you tell me what's bothering you."

That's when I did a huffy breath at him.

'Cos the man wasn't listening to me, of course.

"Yeah, only I already said I can't talk, remember that? 'Cos if I talk, then I might accidentally tell you that my teacher stoled grapes at the supermarket. And then she might have to go to prison. And so that's how come I just have to keep it a secret inside my head. And that's all."

I smoothed my skirt. "The end," I said.

Then I squeezed my lips together very

tight. Or else my secret might slip out.
Only guess what?
I think it already did.

Chapter 7

Sour Grapes

Headteacher called Mrs to come to his office.

Only I didn't even know he was going to do that sneaky thing.

That's how come I had to pull my skirt way over my head. Or else Mrs would see me there. And she would know I told on her.

"Don't do that," said Headteacher.

"Yeah, only I'm allowed," I said from underneath my skirt. "'Cos I have on my new red tights. And also my shorts."

After that, Headteacher went out of his

office. And I heard my teacher's voice outside the door.

Then I quick got down from my big wood chair. And I hided under Headteacher's giant desk. 'Cos I was scared of what was going to happen, that's why.

I stayed quiet for lots of minutes.

Then I heard feet come back in the office. And so I made my breath very quiet.

"Junie? Junie B. Jones?" said Headteacher.

"She might be hiding," said Mrs. "She's good at that, you know."

And so just then I had to think of something very quick. Or else they might come looking for me, I think.

"Yeah, only Junie B. Jones isn't hiding," I said in a scary voice. "Junie B. Jones had to go home. Only don't call her mother. Or else she

will go mad at you and crack your head open."

After that, feet walked real fast around the desk. It was Headteacher.

"Come out of there right now, young lady," he said.

I peeked my eyes at him.

"Drat," I said very quiet.

Then I had to sit in the big wood chair again. And Mrs sat down next to me. Except for I didn't look at her. Or else she might be making a fist at me.

"Good afternoon, Junie B.," she said

in a nice voice.

I did a gulp.

"I think you and I need to have a little talk," she said.

Then my eyes got a teeny bit of wet in them. 'Cos a little talk means I'm gonna get yelled at.

"Yeah, only I tried not to telltale on you," I said very quick. "'Cos I didn't want you to go to prison for stealing grapes. And so I kept it a secret inside my head. And I didn't talk. And Grandma Miller thought a dead cat got my tongue.

"Only today Lucille said my head was gonna blow up. And so that's how come I runned to the nurse for a plaster. And she tooked me to Headteacher. And then my secret accidentally slipped out of my lips."

Mrs dried my eyes with a tissue.

"It's OK, Junie B.," she said. "I'm not angry at you. I just need to know what you saw me do at the supermarket. Can you tell me what you saw?"

Then she said the word *egg-zactly*.

I made my voice very whispering. "I egg-zactly saw you eat grapes," I told her. "Except for you didn't pay for them. You just put them in your mouth and ate them. And that is called the word of stealing, I think."

After that I hided my head under my skirt again.

"You don't have to hide, Junie B.," said Mrs. "*I'm* the one who should be hiding. *I'm* the one who took the grapes."

I peeked my eyes over my skirt at her.

Then Mrs did a little smile. And she explained all about what happened.

"Two weeks ago I bought some grapes at

the supermarket," she said. "But when I got them home I discovered they were so sour no one in my family would eat them.

"So *this* week – when my husband and I went back to the supermarket – I thought I'd be smart and taste a couple of grapes before I bought them."

I raised my eyebrows. "Is that the rules?" I asked very quiet.

Mrs shook her head.

"No," she said. "That's *not* the rules. I should have told the shop man about my sour grapes. And then I should have asked him if I could sample one or two. But I didn't do that. And it was right of you to worry when you saw me eating them without paying for them."

"It was?" I asked.

Mrs smiled again. "Of course it was," she said. "It shows you know right from wrong.

And it also shows that teachers make mistakes just like everybody else. Teachers aren't perfect, Junie B. *No* one is perfect."

After that I felt relief in me. 'Cos of no more secret, that's why.

"Yeah, and guess what else I saw?" I said very happy. "I saw you and your strange man do a big smoochie kiss. And it was right in front of the whole entire everybody! Only you didn't even know I was spying on you! 'Cos I'm not actually allowed to do that sneaky thing. Only my mother never even finded out!"

I smiled very proud of myself.

Except for Mrs didn't smile back.

And Headteacher didn't smile back, too.

'Cos guess why?

Another secret just slipped out.

That's why.

Chapter 8

Grandparents' Day

Mrs went back to Room Nine. That's because the bell rang for Assembly, of course.

Only Headteacher didn't let me go too.

He said to stay in my wood chair.

Then he called Mother on the telephone. And he told her all about the supermarket. And also about my sneaky peeky spying.

Headteacher is a telltale.

After that, Mother said she wanted to talk to me. Only when I said hi, she didn't even say hi back.

She said she wasn't very happy with me, madam. And no more spying means no more spying. And we would talk about this after her work.

Then Mother said she never wants to get any more phone calls from Headteacher. Did I understand? Did I? Did I?

I looked at Headteacher.

"Mother says not to call her any more," I told him.

Then Mother did a loud groan in the phone. Except I don't know why.

After that, me and her hanged up. And Headteacher said I could go to Assembly. And so I runned there speedy quick.

Only too bad for me. 'Cos I got there too late to sing "All things bright and beautiful, All teachers great and small." Which is my favourite song.

And so I just had to sit down at my table in Room Nine, and that's all.

I showed Lucille my plaster.

"See? My head's not blowed up," I said very happy.

"Too bad," said a mean boy named Jim.

I made a fist at him.

Then me and him got into a scuffle.

Scuffle is the school word for I accidentally tore his shirt.

Only guess what? I didn't even get in trouble!

'Cos just then the grandparents came to Room Nine for Grandparents' Day!

"HEY! THERE'S MINE! THERE'S MINE!" I shouted very excited. "MINE IS THE GRAMPA WITH THE BALDIE HEAD!"

"Mine too!" said a girl named Charlotte.

"Mine too!" said my boyfriend named Ricardo.

Then a grandma with blonde hair came in. And she had on long red fingernails. And dangling earrings with jewels on them.

"That's my nanna!" said Lucille.

I smiled at her. "Your nanna looks like a moneybags, Lucille," I said.

After that, another grandma came in. And she runned over to that Jim I hate. And she tried to hug him very tight.

Only that mean Jim just kept on standing there. And he didn't even hug her back.

I tapped on her.

"I will hug you," I said.

And so then me and her hugged real tight.

"I hate your grandboy," I said very sweet.

Just then Mrs clapped her loud hands together. And she made the grandparents sit

61

down in the back of the room.

Then the children talked all about what we do in Room Nine.

"It is fun here," said my bestest friend, that Grace. "We learn to count. And to read. And to wash our hands after we go to the toilet."

"And we learn playtime and snacks and art," said Ricardo.

"Art is my favourite," I called out. "Only my art didn't get hanged up. 'Cos I painted a horse. And his head turned out like a fat sausage. And so I had to tear it up and stomp on it with my shoes."

Then that mean Jim did a duh-brain sign at me.

And it was right in front of the whole entire grandparents!

"Yeah, only everybody makes mistakes!" I

said. "Right, Mrs? Right? 'Cos on Saturday you kissed a strange man at the supermarket. And then you stoled a bunch of grapes. And so even teachers make mistakes. Right?"

Mrs's face went funny. Then her skin turned the colour of reddish. And her voice couldn't say any words.

"How come you're not talking, Mrs?" I called out. "Does the dead cat got your tongue?"

Just then Grandma Miller made a loud laugh at the back of the room.

Then I heard my grampa laugh, too.

And pretty soon, lots of other grand-parents were laughing and laughing.

"HEY! IT SOUNDS HAPPY IN THIS PLACE!" I yelled.

After that, Mrs didn't look so reddish any more.

Then we got out the 'freshments. And Grandma Miller helped me put my biscuits on a plate.

Mrs made a 'nouncement to Room Nine. And she said only two biscuits each for the children.

Except for I ate four delicious chocolate ones. And nobody even saw me!

Only that's not called stealing.

That's called *extras*.

After the 'freshments, the grandparents had to go home to their houses.

And so I hugged my grandma and grandpa very much.

And then I hugged that mean Jim's grandma too.

And also Lucille's moneybags nanna.

"Love your earrings," I said.

Then Mrs saw me being polite. And she smiled very nice at me.

Mrs has white teeth.

They are just like Grampa Miller's teeth. Only hers don't come out, I think.

Except I'm not positive.

And so guess what?

I still wish I could hide in her basket.

That's what.

About the Author

Has Barbara Park done any sneaky peeky spying of her own? "I used to hide in the clothes basket a lot when I was little," she admits. "The smell was not good in there!" Now she follows shop detectives around, watching them nab shoplifters. "I may look like an ordinary customer," she jokes, "but I'm on the case!"

The author of lots of hilarious books for young readers, Barbara Park has received many awards, including seven *Children's Choice* awards and four *Parents' Choice* awards. She lives in Arizona, USA with her husband, Richard, and their two sons, Steven and David.

Junie B. Jones' personal Beeswax

Things I like and things I don't
by Junie B. Jones

I LIKE:

Mrs

I wish Mrs lived next door to me. Then me and her would be neighbours. And bestest friends. And also I could spy on her.

Spying
I am a very good spier. That's because I have sneaky feet. And my nose doesn't whistle when I breathe.

The supermarket
It is very fun at that place. My favourite aisle is where the biscuits are.

The water fountain
I'm almost five years old so I already know how to work this thing.

Art
It's my favourite, only my art didn't get hanged up. 'Cos I painted a horse. And his head turned out like a fat sausage.

Gold stars

I DISLIKE:

Bedtime
My bedtime is when the little hand is at the seven, and the big hand is at the six. Only I hate that stupid bedtime. 'Cos I'm not even tired yet.

Little talks
A little talk is when Mother is mad at me. And she says who do I thing I am, madam?

Stupid stinky vegetables
Yucky blucky brockly, euwie pewie tomatoes, and Archie Chokes.

Big smoochie kisses

Joking Around with Junie B.!

What is the longest word in the dictionary?
The word SMILES because there is a MILE between each S.

Why did the chicken cross the playground?
To get to the other SLIDE.

What happened to the dog that swallowed a fire-fly?
It barked with de-light!

What did the blanket say to the bed?
Let's go undercover.

Knock, knock
Who's there?
Kook
Kook who?
Hey! Who are you calling a cuckoo?

Read this next book about me. And I mean it!

The bestest girl is a winner

First, I got the sponge from under the sink. Then I made it soaky wet with water. I pointed it at the target.

"Ready . . . aim . . . fire!" I said.

Then I throwed the sponge with all my might.

It splashed right in the middle of the toilet bowl!

"BULL'S-EYE! I MADE A BULL'S EYE" I shouted very excited.

But just then, I heard a knock at the door. It was Mother!

"OPEN UP RIGHT NOW, YOUNG LADY! she yelled.